A Bag of Moonshine

Also by Alan Garner

A BAG OF MOONSHINE

Alan Garner

Illustrations by Patrick James Lynch

DELACORTE PRESS/NEW YORK

Published by
Delacorte Press
1 Dag Hammarskjold Plaza
New York, NY 10017

Published simultaneously in Great Britain by William Collins
Sons & Co. Ltd.

Manufactured in Singapore

First U.S.A. printing

Library of Congress Cataloging-in-Publication Data

Garner, Alan.
   A bag of moonshine.
   6 |89
   Summary: Twenty-two folktales from various parts of the
British Isles.
   1. Tales—Great Britain.   [1. Folklore—Great Britain]
I. Lynch, Patrick James, ill.   II. Title.
PZ8.1.G167Bag 1986   398.2'1'0941
ISBN 0-385-29517-0
Library of Congress Catalog Card Number: 86-13382

J
398.2
GAR

Contents

for
Wilfred Lancaster
*

and
for
Joshua Birtles
Fred Wright
Tom Turnock
Dafydd Rees

IN MEMORIAM

" – it is in the speech of carters and housewives, in the speech of blacksmiths and old women, that one discovers the magic that sings the claim of the voice in the shadow, or that chants the rhyme of the fish in the well."

JOHN MARUSKIN

Jack My Lad

Jack was a boy that sold buttermilk, and one day, as he went along, he met a witch.

"Jack, my lad," said the witch, "sell me a bit of your buttermilk."

"No," said Jack. "I shall not."

"If you don't," said the witch, "I'll put you in my sack."

"No," said Jack. "Not a drop," said Jack. "You can't have any; and that's that."

So the witch put Jack in her sack, the sack on her back, and set off for home. After a while, she said, "Eh up. I was forgetting. I'll want some fat to fry with."

"Then you'd best let me down, missis," said Jack, "and go fetch your fat. I'm too big to carry to the shop."

"If I do that," said the witch, "you'll run away."

"No, I'll never," said Jack.

The witch saw some men who were cutting a thorn tree; and she said to them, "Just you keep an eye on this sack for me while I go fetch some fat to fry with."

"Right you are, missis," said the men. "We'll keep an eye on your sack."

So the witch left the sack with the men, and off she went to fetch her fat.

As soon as she was gone, "Now then," said Jack. "You let us out, and I'll give you some buttermilk." Well, the men let Jack out, and he gave them some buttermilk, and he said, "I know what. Fill this here sack up with the thorns you've been cutting, and I'll get off home."

So the men filled the sack with the thorns, and Jack went home. And along comes the witch with the fat, takes the sack full of thorns, sets the sack on her back, and off she goes.

Well, it wasn't long before those thorns began to prick her, and the witch, she said, "I reckon you've got pins in your pocket, Jack, my lad. I mustn't forget to take them out when I'm frying." But when she got to her house and opened the sack and tipped the thorns onto a clean white sheet, she said, "Well, I'll be jiggered! Jack, my lad, I'm going to catch you, and then I'm going to boil you; and that's a fact."

The next day, Jack met the witch again.

"Jack, my lad," said the witch, "sell me a bit of your buttermilk."

"No," said Jack. "I shall not."

"If you don't," said the witch, "I'll put you in my sack."

"No," said Jack. "Not a drop," said Jack. "You can't have any; and that's that."

So the witch put Jack in her sack, the sack on her back, and set off for home. After a while, she said, "Eh up. I was forgetting. I'll want some salt to boil with."

"Then you'd best let me down, missis," said Jack, "and go fetch your salt. I'm too big to carry to the shop."

"If I do that," said the witch, "you'll run away."

"No, I'll never," said Jack.

The witch saw some men who were digging a hole; and she said to them, "Just you keep an eye on this sack for me while I go fetch some salt to boil with."

"Right you are, missis," said the men. "We'll keep an eye on your sack."

So the witch left the sack with the men, and off she went to fetch her salt.

As soon as she was gone, "Now then," said Jack. "You let us out, and I'll give you some buttermilk." Well, the men let Jack out, and he gave them some buttermilk, and he said, "I know what. Fill this here

sack up with the stones you've been digging, and I'll get off home."

So the men filled the sack with the stones, and Jack went home. And along comes the witch with the salt, takes the sack full of stones, sets the sack on her back, and off she goes.

Well, it wasn't long before the stones began to rattle, and the witch, she said, "My lad Jack, your bones do crack!" But when she got to her house and opened the sack and tipped the stones onto a clean white sheet, she said, "Well, I'll be jiggered! Jack, my lad, I'm going to catch you, and then I'm going to roast you; and that's a fact."

The next day, Jack met the witch again.

"Jack, my lad," said the witch, "sell me a bit of your buttermilk."

"No," said Jack. "I shall not."

"If you don't," said the witch, "I'll put you in my sack."

"No," said Jack. "Not a drop," said Jack. "You can't have any; and that's that."

So the witch put Jack in her sack, the sack on her back, and set off for home. And when she got to her house, the witch said to her cat, "Just you keep an eye on this sack for me, while I fetch sticks for the fire."

The witch left the sack with the cat, and locked the

door behind her while she fetched sticks for the fire.

As soon as she was gone, "Now then," said Jack. "You let us out, and I'll give you some buttermilk." Well, the cat let Jack out, and he gave it some buttermilk; and after that, he filled the sack with every pot in the witch's scullery. Then he ran up the flue, down the roof and all the way back to his own house.

The witch came in with the sticks. She lit the fire, opened the sack, tipped the pots onto a clean white sheet, and broke them every single one.

"Well, I'll be jiggered!" said the witch. "Jack, my lad!" she shouted up the chimney. "Keep your buttermilk, you great nowt! And never again come near me!"

And he never did.

Mr Vinegar

Mr and Mrs Vinegar lived in a vinegar bottle, and one day Mrs Vinegar was sweeping the house so hard she broke it all to bits.

"Eh dear," said Mr Vinegar when he came home. "Smashed to smithereens. But never mind." And he picked up the door of the house, and set it on his back and marched off with Mrs Vinegar into the world to mend their fortunes.

After a while, they came to a wood, and a thick dark wood it was, too, by all accounts, with wolves and bears and suchlike in it; and Mr and Mrs Vinegar didn't fancy spending the night there; they did not. So they marched up into a tree, with their door, and settled themselves to sleep in the branches.

Well, they hadn't been there long when what should happen but a gang of robbers sat down at the bottom of the tree and started to share out the money they'd got from robbing people and cutting their throats.

16

"Here's a guinea for you," one was saying, and, "No, it isn't," says another, "that's mine;" and another, "It never is," he says, "just you give it here!" and so on, till they were fighting and making such a row that Mr and Mrs Vinegar, up in the tree, didn't know what to do. They shook and they shook. They trembled and they trembled; and they trembled the door right out of the tree down onto the robbers' heads; and the robbers, they ran off, half scared to death.

But Mr and Mrs Vinegar didn't dare to come down from that tree until daylight. Then Mr Vinegar picked up the door to set it on his back and march off to mend their fortunes; and what should he see under that door but a heap of golden guineas that the robbers had left behind them.

"Eh dear," said Mr Vinegar. "What a performance."

"My stars and garters and little apples!" said Mrs Vinegar. "You take these golden guineas and buy us a cow, and that will set us up for life."

So Mr Vinegar took the golden guineas, and he went to the market to buy him a cow. And he bought a cow: a fine, red cow in full milk it was. He handed over the golden guineas, and he drove the cow back along the road to show to his wife.

Well, he hadn't gone far when he met a man playing bagpipes, and all the children were following him and dancing.

"Eh dear," said Mr Vinegar. "I do wish I had those
bagpipes, and then. But never mind."

"You can have these bagpipes," said the man, "if
you'll give me your red cow."

"Done!" said Mr Vinegar. And he gave the man
the red cow, and the man gave him the bagpipes, and
Mr Vinegar marched off down the road, the children
following. But Mr Vinegar had never learned to play
on bagpipes, nor on anything else, for that matter,
and the children soon began to laugh at him and his

caterwauling. They didn't dance any more, either, and Mr Vinegar's fingers grew stiff and cold with trying to play.

"Eh dear," said Mr Vinegar. "I do wish I had a pair of gloves to warm me, and then. But never mind."

"You can have my gloves," said a man on the road, "if you'll give me your bagpipes."

"Done!" said Mr Vinegar. And he gave the man the bagpipes, and Mr Vinegar put the gloves on and marched off to show them to his wife.

By this time it was getting late, and Mr Vinegar was tired, and when he saw a man coming towards him with a good stout stick in his hand, Mr Vinegar said, "Eh dear. I do wish I had a good stout stick in my hand to lean on, and then. But never mind."

"You can have my stick," said the man, "if you'll give me your gloves."

"Done!" said Mr Vinegar. The man took the gloves, and Mr Vinegar took the stick and he marched off to show it to his wife.

Now there was a parrot sitting in a tree, and when

it saw Mr Vinegar on the road it laughed, and said, "You rum cove! You could have got that stick from any hedge. Where are your golden guineas now?"

"You get off with your bother!" said Mr Vinegar; and he was so vexed he threw the stick at the parrot; but he missed, and the stick lodged fast in the tree where he couldn't reach it, and the parrot flew away, laughing.

So, with no cow, no bagpipes, no gloves, and no stick, either, Mr Vinegar went back to his wife. But Mrs Vinegar, didn't she give him some stick, after? What! She did that! I'll say she did! She gave him stick all right, and no error!

Grey Goat

Once upon a time there was a grey goat, and she had three kids. She went to the forest to fetch wood for the stove, and when she came back the kids had gone. They were not in the house. They were not in the field. So the grey goat set out to find them.

She met a gull on a rock, and she said:

> "Here am I,
> a grey goat.
> Lost are my kind kids.
> Back and to I go.
> Dark is the night
> till I find them."

But the gull said:

> "By earth that is under,
> by air that is over,
> I have not seen your kids."

The grey goat went on, until she met a crow at a gate, and she said:

21

A Bag of Moonshine

"Here am I,
a grey goat.
Lost are my kind kids.
Back and to I go.
Dark is the night
till I find them."

But the crow said:

"By earth that is under,
by air that is over,
I have not seen your kids."

So the grey goat went on, until she came to the house of a fox; and she stood on the roof. The fox looked out of the window, and said:

"It grows dim here.
My pot will not boil.
My cake will not bake.
My child will not go to the well.
Who is on top?"

And the grey goat said:

"Here am I,
a grey goat.
Lost are my kind kids.
Back and to I go.
Dark is the night
till I find them."

But the fox said:

> "By thorn and by fire,
> by earth that is under,
> by star and by storm,
> I have not seen your kids."

The grey goat said, "Even so, let me in." So the fox let her in. And the grey goat looked all around, and said:

> "No food on the shelf.
> No meal in the pot.
> Yet here's a fat fox,
> not a lean one."

And the fox said again:

> "By thorn and by fire,
> by earth that is under,
> by star and by storm,
> I have not seen your kids.
> Never. Never.
> I have not seen your kids."

But the grey goat looked all around, and said:

> "No food on the shelf – "

And a voice called out, "Mother!"
And the grey goat said:

> "No meal in the pot – "

24

Grey Goat

And a voice called out, "Mother! Mother!"
And the grey goat said:

"Yet here's a fat fox,
not a lean one!"

And a voice called out, "Mother! Mother! Mother!"
Then the grey goat took an axe, and killed the fox;
and inside the fox were the three kids; and they threw
the fox onto the midden and all went home together.

Now it would be fine indeed if there were more;
but there is not.

Tom Poker

One winter's day, Tom Poker went out chopping wood. (It was a hard winter, and times were bad.)

He'd not gone far when he trod on some ice; and he slipped and he fell, and it took his breath away. Tom Poker said to the ice, "Ice, ice," said Tom Poker, "you've knocked me down. You must be strong."

"I am," said the ice. "You may depend on it."

"But when sun comes, you run away," said Tom Poker.

"Oh," said the ice, "that's very true."

"Well, then," said Tom Poker; "sun is stronger."

And the ice said, "He is, seemingly."

Tom Poker said to the sun, "Sun, sun," said Tom Poker, "are you strong?"

"I am," said the sun. "You may depend on it."

"But when cloud comes, you hide," said Tom Poker.

Tom Poker

"Oh," said the sun, "that's very true."

"Well, then," said Tom Poker; "cloud is stronger."

And the sun said, "She is, seemingly."

Tom Poker said to the cloud, "Cloud, cloud," said Tom Poker, "are you strong?"

"I am," said the cloud. "You may depend on it."

"But when wind comes, you're blown to bits," said Tom Poker.

"Oh," said the cloud, "that's very true."

"Well, then," said Tom Poker; "wind is stronger."

And the cloud said, "She is, seemingly."

Tom Poker said to the wind, "Wind, wind," said Tom Poker, "are you strong?"

"I am," said the wind. "You may depend on it."

"But can you shift hill?" said Tom Poker.

"I can't," said the wind. "That's very true."

"Well, then," said Tom Poker; "hill is stronger."

And the wind said, "He is, seemingly."

Tom Poker said to the hill, "Hill, hill," said Tom Poker, "are you strong?"

"I am," said the hill. "You may depend on it."

"But can you stand on tree?" said Tom Poker.

"I can't," said the hill.

"But tree can stand on you," said Tom Poker.

"She can," said the hill. "That's very true."

"Well, then," said Tom Poker; "tree is stronger."

And the hill said, "She is, seemingly."

Tom Poker

Tom Poker said to the tree, "Tree, tree," said Tom Poker, "are you strong?"

"I am," said the tree. "You may depend on it."

Tom Poker swung his axe. "Then have that! and have that! and have that!" said Tom Poker. "Have that! And now who is strong?" said Tom Poker.

But the tree said never a word; for he'd chopped the tree down.

"Me, seemingly! Strongest of all!" said Tom Poker. And he gave a hop. But he hopped on the ice, and he slipped; and the ice took his breath away from Tom Poker.

Jack and the Boggarts

Jack and his mother kept hens; and one night, thieves came to the house and took twelve pullets and a cockerel, while Jack and his mother slept sound and heard nothing.

"Well!" said Jack's mother in the morning. "The cheek and impudence! Jack," she says, "tonight, you see that you keep an eye on the hencote door."

"Yes, mother," says Jack. "I shall that; never fret."

So, the next night, Jack took the hencote door up to bed with him and had it for his pillow. And the thieves came again, they did, and this time they took all the chickens there were, and left the hencote empty, while Jack and his mother slept sound and heard nothing.

"Well!" says Jack's mother in the morning. "The cheek and impudence! Jack," she says, "I thought I told you to keep an eye on the hencote door last night."

"Yes, mother," says Jack. "And it makes a hard pillow."

"Well!" says Jack's mother. "Sooner than trust you to do the job right, you blunderskull, you big dunce, I'd have you wind rope out of sand!"

"Yes, mother," says Jack. "I shall that; never fret." And Jack went up the road to the sandhole, a big quarry place where people went when they wanted some sand; and he took a load of sand, and he set about winding rope out of it.

Now in this sandhole there lived a boggart; and when he saw Jack winding rope out of the sand, the boggart says, "Whatever are you doing, Jack?"

"I'm winding rope out of sand," says Jack, "to throttle boggarts with who live in our sandhole and won't pay rent."

"Wait on, Jack," says the boggart. "I must go tell my grandad about this." And off went the boggart down the hole, while Jack got on with his winding.

Sooner or later, the boggart came back with a big stick; and he says, "Jack," he says, "Grandad says we'll pay rent if you can chuck his stick higher than I can. And if not, we'll eat you."

"Fair do's," says Jack.

So the boggart threw his grandad's stick into the air, and it went so high that Jack could scarce see it, and when it came down again it went so deep into the ground that Jack could scarce catch hold on it.

"There," says the boggart. "Now it's your turn."

But the stick was so fast in the ground that Jack could scarce shift it.

"Buck up!" says the boggart. "What are you waiting for?"

"I'm waiting for that cloud yonder to come a bit nearer," says Jack; "so as I can chuck the stick on top of it."

"Oh no you don't," says the boggart. "What would grandad do without his stick?" And the boggart pulled the stick out of the ground and went off down the hole, while Jack got on with his winding.

Sooner or later, the boggart came back with a horse, and he says, "Jack," he says, "Grandad says we'll pay rent if you can carry this horse round this here sandhole one more time than I can. And if not, we'll eat you."

"Fair do's," says Jack.

So the boggart picked up the horse, hutched it on his shoulders and set off with it round the sandhole. He carried that horse round that sandhole ten times before he was forced to put it down.

"There," says the boggart. "Now it's your go."

"How must I carry it?" says Jack. "On my shoulder, or between my legs?"

"Between your legs," says the boggart, and he

32

thought: That's done him!

But Jack jumped up on the horse's back, and he rode it round the sandhole; and he rode it and he rode it until that horse was blowing and it couldn't go another step; twenty times round, he went.

The boggart was amazed; and he calls down to his grandad, "He's carried it between his legs!" And the boggart's grandad says, "Best pay him, then!"

"I'm to pay you," says the boggart to Jack. "How much is rent?"

"Oh," says Jack, "I reckon my cap filled with gold will do."

So the boggart went off down the hole to fetch the gold, and, while he was gone, Jack dug a pit, cut the crown from his cap, held his cap over the pit and waited for the boggart.

Sooner or later, the boggart came back with the gold and began at pouring it into Jack's cap; but Jack's cap wasn't filled, and the boggart had to go and fetch more. And he had to fetch more again; but still it wasn't filled.

"Grandad!" says the boggart. "We want more gold for rent!"

"There is none!" says the boggart's grandad. "We've run out!"

"What must we do?" says the boggart.

"Best be flitting!" says the boggart's grandad.

So the boggarts had to flit; and Jack was left with a hole full of sand and a pit full of gold; and Jack's mother, she was very pleased.

Mollyndroat

There was a woman once in the Isle of Man, and she was scandalous lazy. She was that lazy she would do nothing but sit in the corner of the hearth, warming her shinbones red. And one day, her man gives her some wool to spin for him; and he was not what you would call bright. No; he was slow on the uptaking. But even he could see that he was badly off for clothes to wear, for she was letting them get all ragged on him. Now he'd told her to mend them; told her till he was tired; but all he got out of her was: "Time enough. There's time enough."

So, this day, he says to her, "Here's some wool for you to spin," says he. "And if it's not done a month from now, I'll throw you out on the road side, so I will. You and your 'time enough' have left me nearly bare!"

Well, the wife was too lazy to spin, even so, but she pretended to be working hard when the man was

35

in the house; and she put the wheel out on the floor every night before the man came in from the field, to be letting on to him that she'd been spinning.

After a while of seeing the wheel so much, and with a week to go to the reckoning, the man says to the wife, "Have you enough thread spun at you now for me to take to the weaver next week, do you think?"

"I don't know at all," says the wife. "I've not had chance to count the balls, I've been that busy. I put them all in the loft as I spin them."

"Well, let's count them now," says he.

"Very well," says she.

Now she had only the one ball spun, and that was knotted, and rough as gorse; but she took it – and then the play began!

"Keep the count yourself," says she, "and throw them back to me, so they don't get rolling all over the floor."

"I will," says he.

She threw the ball down to him.

"That's one," says he; and he threw it back up to her.

"Here's another," says she; and she threw the ball back down to him.

"That's two," says he.

"It is," says she; and he threw it back up to her.

36

And when they had done that between them maybe two score times, the wife's arms were aching, and she says, "That's all that's in it."

"Oh, indeed you've spun well, woman," says he, "there's plenty done for the weaver. I shall get enough for a suit of clothes in the week."

Well, then she was in a fix, and didn't know in her senses what to do to save herself from being thrown on the road side. She knew she would sup sorrow if she was found out.

At last, she thought there was nothing for it but to go back to ask help of the Foawr that lived up the mountain, on the other side of the dark wood. And in those days there were Foawrs to be found, if you knew how to look, but they were great goblin things that it didn't do to meddle with; so people left them alone. They're all gone now; or let's hope they are.

Anyway, this woman took the road early next morning, as soon as the man was in the field, and carried the wool with her. She walked up hills, and down gills, till at last she came to the Foawr's house.

"What are you wanting here?" says the Foawr.

"I'm wanting you to help me," says she; and she up and told him about the ball of thread and all.

"I'll spin the wool for you," says the Foawr, "if you'll tell me my name a week from this day. Or I keep the wool; and maybe eat you. Will that do?"

"Why should it not?" says the wife, and thinks: It's a queer thing if I can't find out a name in a week. So she left the wool with the Foawr, and went home.

Well, she was wrong. The woman tried every way, but nobody knew the Foawr's name, had ever heard of it, or ever thought that he had one. And time was getting over fast, and she was no nearer an answer.

And then it was the last evening. She sat in the hearth, and wondered whether she was to be eaten, or be thrown in a ditch. It came on dark, and the man was late; but when he tramped in, he was laughing.

"Where have you been?" says she. "Did you hear anything new?"

"Oh," says he, "you think you're good to spin, but I think there's one better than you, for all."

"And who's that?" says she.

"Never in all my born days," says he, "did I see such spinning! Thread as fine as cobweb; and such singing!"

"And where was this?" says she.

"Why," says he, "where but in the Foawr's house tonight! I saw it up on the mountain, all in a blaze of light. And such whirling and whistling coming to my ears! And the singing and laughing and shouting! So I made my way there, and I drew near the window, and there's the big ugsome Foawr inside, sitting at a wheel, spinning like the wind, and his hand flying

like the lightning, and he shouting to the whistling wheel!"

"Shouting what?" says the wife.

"It was the burden of this," says the man:

> "'Spin, wheel, spin! Sing, wheel, sing!
> Every beam on the house, spin overhead!
> The wool is hers, the thread is mine!
> How little knows the lazy wife
> It's Mollyndroat that spins it fine!'"

Well, well, the joy the woman took when she heard her man sing the Foawr's song!

"Ah, sweet music!" says she. "Sing it again, man!"
And he sang it again, till she knew it by heart.

Next morning early, she's away to the Foawr's
house. And as she went through the wood, she sang:

"Spin, wheel, spin; spin, wheel, spin.
Every branch on the tree, spin overhead.
The wool is my man's; the thread is my own;
And old Mollyndroat may whistle for his bone!"

When she got to the house, the door was open before her, so in she went.

"I've come again for the thread," says she.

"Easy, easy, woman," says the Foawr. "If you don't tell my name, you don't get the thread; that was the bargain." And, says he, "Now, what is my name?"

"Is it Mollyrea?" says she.

"It is not," says he.

"Are you a Mollyrui?" says she.

"They're not my lot," says he.

"Are they calling you Mollyvridey?" says she.

"They are not," says he.

"I'll warrant your name is Mollychreest," says she.

"You are wrong," says he.

"Are you going by the name of Mollyvoirrey?" says she.

"Indeed I am not," says he.

"Maybe your name is Mollyvarten," says she.

"And maybe it's not, at all," says he.

"Well," says she, "there was only seven families living here in the old time, and their names were all 'Molly' at the front. And so," says she, "if you're not

42

a Mollycharaine – "

"I am not," says he.

"Then," says she, "you're not one of the real, old, proper families, at all."

"I am not," says he. "And now," says he, "be careful, woman. I'm tired of the playing. Your next guess is your last."

But she pointed her finger at him, the woman did, and says, slowly:

"The wool is my man's. The thread is my own.
Old Mollyndroat may whistle for his bone!"

Well, the Foawr, he was done, and he was in a red rage, and he cries, "Bad luck to you! You never would have come on my name if you're not a witch!"

"Bad luck to you, my boy," says she, "for trying to steal a decent woman's wool!"

"You and your witchings!" shouts he, and he flung the balls of thread at her and ran out, howling.

And away home with her, and her balls of thread. And if she didn't spin her own wool for ever after, that's nothing to do with you and me.

The Three Gowks

Once upon a time, when I was young and handsome, and that hasn't been so very long ago, as you can see, there was an old couple lived on a nice bit of land of their own; and they had a daughter called Matilda, and she was waiting to be wedded to a youth called Tom.

Now there was a garden to the back of the house where they lived, with a well in it; and one day, the old man was walking in the garden when he sees the well, and "Oh!" he says. "If Tom should take our Tilda, and Tilda should have a child, and the child should go tittle-tottle by the well, and fall in, what a thing that would be!" And he sat himself down, and he began to weep.

Up comes the old woman, and sees him, and she says, "What's upsetting you?" And he says, "I was thinking. If Tom should take Tilda, and Tilda should have a child, and the child should go tittle-tottle by

44

the well, and fall in, what a thing that would be!"

"Oh, it would and all!" says the old woman. "Oh,
the little mite, bless him!" So she sat down; and she
began to weep, too.

Up comes Matilda next, and sees the pair of them, and she says, "What's all the skriking about?"

Her mother and father put their arms round her, and they say, "We were thinking! If Tom should take Tilda, and Tilda should have a child, and the child should go tittle-tottle by the well, and fall in, what a thing that would be!"

And Matilda, she bursts into tears, and she says, "Oh, my poor baby!" And there the three of them sat, skriking their eyes out.

Just then, Tom comes by. "Hello," he says.

"Oh!" says Matilda. "We've been thinking!"

"Have you?" says Tom. "What about?"

"If Tom should take Tilda!" says the old man.

"And Tilda should have a child!" says the old woman.

"And the child should go tittle-tottle by the well, and fall in !" says Matilda.

"What a thing that would be!" they all say; and off they go again.

"Well," says Tom, "I know what to do to save the child's life."

"Oh, tell us!" they say, all three of them.

"I'm going to put on a new pair of shoes," says Tom, "and I'm going to set off walking; and if, by the time those shoes are worn out, I've not met three gowks as big as you, I'll save the child's life."

"How?" says Matilda.

"By not marrying you!" says Tom to her.

So he put on a new pair of shoes, Tom did, and he took his stick, and he set off walking.

It was a nice day, and he'd not gone very far, when he came to a barn with its two doors wide open, and a man there shovelling with a big shovel; but what he was shovelling, Tom couldn't see, for there was nothing there to shovel.

"What are you doing, master?" says Tom.

"I'm shovelling sunshine over my sheaves," says the man. "Yesterday it rained, and we were forced to get them in the wet."

"Would you not do better," says Tom, "to carry your wheat out and lay it in the sun?"

"I wish you'd come this way sooner," says the man. "You'd have saved me hours of my time."

"That's one gowk," says Tom to himself; and he cut a notch in his stick.

He went a bit further, and he saw a man by the road side, hunched up, hacking at pebbles with a knife.

"And what are you doing, master?" says Tom.

"I'm cutting pebbles," says the man, "to get at the kernels."

"Would you not do better," says Tom, "to take a mason's hammer to them, first, and split them, and then see whether they've kernels or no?"

"I wish you'd come sooner," says the man. "Many a good knife you'd have saved me, if you'd come this way before."

"That's two gowks," says Tom to himself; and he cut another notch in his stick.

He left the man by the road side, but, round the next bend, he saw another; and this one was pulling on a rope. The rope went over the roof of a house and down the other side, and the end was tied to a

cow's neck. The cow was on its hind legs up the wall and blahting fit to bring a sick man sorrow and a dead man woe.

"What's going on here, master?" says Tom. "Aren't you feared you'll maul your belly out?"

"I'm shaping to get this cow on the roof," says the man, "so as it can eat that grass that's growing in the thatch."

"Would you not do better," says Tom, "to fetch your ladder and go up on the roof yourself, and cut the grass and chuck it down?"

"I wish you'd come this way sooner," says the man. "You'd have saved me many a cow I've throttled, if you'd come this way before."

"That's the three," says Tom; and he cut a third notch in his stick. "Time I was gone home."

And he turned, and he went back home to Matilda.

Tom wore the shoes to his wedding, for they were still new, and scarce broken in, even. Then, sure enough, Matilda and Tom had a child; but, before it could walk, Tom, he'd taught it to swim. He had that!

A Fat Hen

A fat hen.

Two ducks
And a fat hen.

Three plump partridge
Two ducks
And a fat hen.

Four hairy herrings,
Three plump partridge,
Two ducks
And a fat hen.

Five white weasels,
Four hairy herrings,
Three plump partridge,
Two ducks
And a fat hen.

Six screeching wild geese,
Five white weasels,
Four hairy herrings,
Three plump partridge,
Two ducks
and a fat hen.

Seven bottles of mountain ash,
Six screeching wild geese,
Five white weasels,
Four hairy herrings,
Three plump partridge,
Two ducks
And a fat hen.

Eight dozen Limerick oysters,
Seven bottles of mountain ash,
Six screeching wild geese,
Five white weasels,
Four hairy herrings,
Three plump partridge,
Two ducks
And a fat hen.

Nine peevish parsons in a purple pulpit preaching,
Eight dozen Limerick oysters,
Seven bottles of mountain ash,
Six screeching wild geese,
Five white weasels,
Four hairy herrings,
Three plump partridge,
Two ducks
And a fat hen.

Ten crooked crows in a crooked crab tree croaking,
Nine peevish parsons in a purple pulpit preaching,
Eight dozen Limerick oysters,
Seven bottles of mountain ash,
Six screeching wild geese,
Five white weasels,
Four hairy herrings,
Three plump partridge,
Two ducks
And a fat hen.

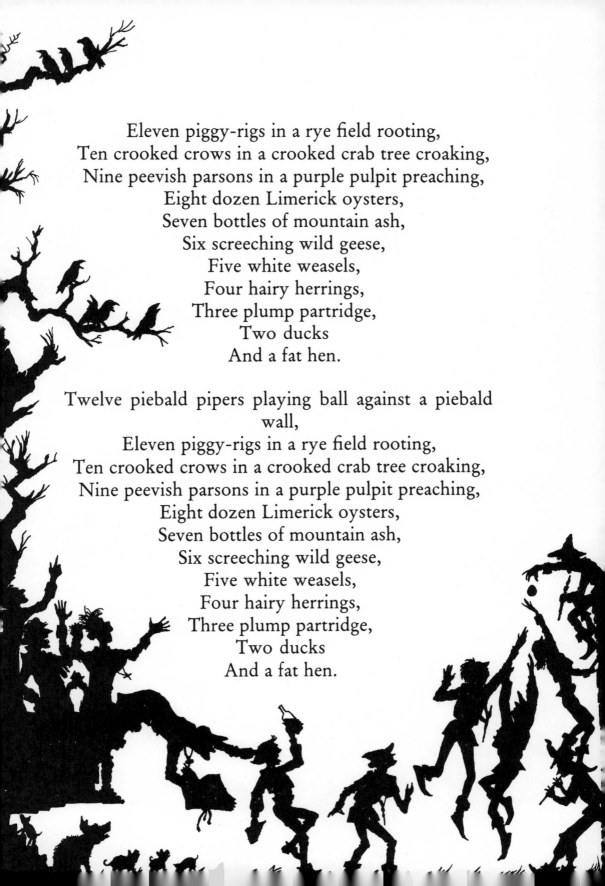

Eleven piggy-rigs in a rye field rooting,
Ten crooked crows in a crooked crab tree croaking,
Nine peevish parsons in a purple pulpit preaching,
Eight dozen Limerick oysters,
Seven bottles of mountain ash,
Six screeching wild geese,
Five white weasels,
Four hairy herrings,
Three plump partridge,
Two ducks
And a fat hen.

Twelve piebald pipers playing ball against a piebald
wall,
Eleven piggy-rigs in a rye field rooting,
Ten crooked crows in a crooked crab tree croaking,
Nine peevish parsons in a purple pulpit preaching,
Eight dozen Limerick oysters,
Seven bottles of mountain ash,
Six screeching wild geese,
Five white weasels,
Four hairy herrings,
Three plump partridge,
Two ducks
And a fat hen.

Jack and the Beekeeper

If you don't like, don't listen; but there were once three brothers; two were clever, and one was Jack. Anyway; they went to a wood, and they wanted to eat their dinners there; so they filled a pot with porridge oats and water; and then what must they do for a fire?

Well, not far off, they saw a beekeeper's house, and, "I know what," says the oldest brother. "You two fetch sticks, and I'll go get us some fire from the beekeeper yonder."

So he went to the beekeeper, and he says, "Now then, Dad," he says, "let's be having a bit of fire to make porridge with, me and my two brothers."

"Right-ho," says the beekeeper. "But sing us a song first."

"Song?" says the oldest brother. "I don't know any songs."

"Well, dance for us, then," says the beekeeper.

"I don't know any dances, neither," says the oldest brother.

"No song and no dances," says the beekeeper. "Well, you're a right one! Get away with your bother! You'll have no fire from me!"

And he sent him packing.

"What?" says the next brother, when the oldest got back. "No light? We'll soon see about that!" And off he went to the beekeeper's house.

"Now then, Dad," says he, "Let's be having a bit of fire to make porridge with, me and my two brothers."

"Right-ho," says the beekeeper. "But give us a song first."

"What?" says he. "Me sing? I've no songs!"

"You can tell us a tale, then," says the beekeeper.

"I've no tales, neither."

"No song and no tale," says the beekeeper. "Then you've no fire! Get away with your bother!" And he sent him packing.

So that one, he went back. And there the brothers were, the pair of them, staring like stuck pigs, and no fire.

"Well," says Jack, "you've not got much light between you, have you? Let's see what the little un can do."

And off he goes to the beekeeper's house.

"Now then, Dad," says Jack, "can you let us have a bit of fire to cook porridge with, me and my two brothers?"

"Right-ho," says the beekeeper. "But shall you dance first?"

"Oh dear," says Jack. "I can't dance, me."

"Well, what can you do?" says the beekeeper.

"I can tell a tale," says Jack. "That I can. And if I cause you to stop me, Dad," he says, "before I've done my telling, I'll take your fire for my porridge. Do you get my meaning?"

"Oh, I do," says the beekeeper.

"Not a word," says Jack.

"Not a word," says the beekeeper; and he sat with his bald patch to the sun.

"Right," says Jack. "Now you listen."

"I'm listening, youth," says the beekeeper. "I'm listening, my light."

"Time was," says Jack, "I had a piebald horse. And I used to take this horse into the wood to go logging. And one morning, I set off, with me riding on the horse's back, and my axe stuck in my belt. Well, the horse began to trot: trot, trot, trot it went. And there's me on top, going same as bump, bump, bump, up and down; and my axe in my belt, going thump, thump, thump. And what with bumping and thumping, thumping and bumping, that axe bumped and thumped the horse's rump right off him, it did. It thumped it clean off. Are you listening, Dad?"

And Jack slapped the beekeeper on his bald patch with his glove.

"I'm listening, youth," says the beekeeper. "I'm listening, my light."

"Well," says Jack, "I rode that piebald horse on its front legs for three years. Then what should I come on but the horse's rump, bold as ninepence, standing in the meadow and nibbling grass. So I catched it, and stitched it back on to the front of the horse. And I rode it for another three years. Are you listening, Dad?"

And Jack slapped the beekeeper on his bald patch with his glove.

"I'm listening, youth," says the beekeeper. "I'm listening, my light."

"I rode and I rode," says Jack, "and I come to a great oak tree. And I climbed that oak tree right up to the sky. And when I got to the sky, I found that, up there, cows were coming cheap, and flies were very dear. So I went back down to the ground, and I catched two sacks of flies, put them on my shoulders, and climbed up again. And, for every one of those flies, I got a cow and a calf from the farmers up there. Are you listening, Dad?"

And Jack slapped the beekeeper on his bald patch with his glove.

"I'm listening, youth," says the beekeeper. "I'm listening, my light."

"Well," says Jack, "there I was, with this herd of cows in the sky. And I went to drive them back home. But when I got to the oak tree, blow me if some beggar hadn't been and chopped it down! So I took all my cows, and I killed them, and I got all their hides, and I made them into one big long strap; and I let it down from the sky. Then I set off, sliding down this strap. And I slid and I slid, till I slid right off the end almost; but I was short a piece, about as long as from here to my brothers. Are you listening, Dad?"

And Jack slapped the beekeeper on his bald patch with his glove.

"I'm listening, youth," says the beekeeper. "I'm listening, my light."

"Well," says Jack, "I durstn't jump. But just then, a chap in the fields below started winnowing his grain; and the husks, they flew up, and I catched them, and I began at plaiting a rope of them. And I tied this rope on the end of the strap, and I was making to climb down, when a wind came along and blew me, first this road, and then that, back and to, back and to, like a dog at a fair, till the rope had to break, and down I plopped into a boggy patch of marsh, and I sank in this marsh up to my neck. What should happen but a duck come and built its nest in my hair, and if it didn't lay two eggs in it! So there I was: nest on my head, me in the marsh; when up came a fox, sees the eggs, and thinks he'll have them. But no sooner did he reach me than I grabbed his tail, and set up such a commotion, tantivy! tantivy! screaming and yelling, that that fox thought the hounds were at him, and off he goes, and pulls me right out of the marsh. Are you listening, Dad?"

And Jack slapped the beekeeper on his bald patch with his glove.

"I'm listening, youth," says the beekeeper. "I'm listening, my light."

"No matter of that," says Jack, "but who should come next but my grandad, riding piggyback on your grandad."

"No, he never! Oh no, he did not!" says the beekeeper. "It was my grandad riding piggy on yours!"

At that, Jack laughed, and he upped and took the fire and ran off with it, still laughing.

So Jack and his two brothers put the pot on the fire. And when the porridge is cooked, we'll go on with the tale. But just for now, we'll let it simmer.

The Salmon Cariad

There was a Welsh youth went fishing on a river one moonlight night. He sat in his coracle, as they call it, and he had his paddle tucked under his arm, and he was holding on to his rod and the knocker for killing the fish, all at the same time, when a great salmon jumped up and took the fly.

The coracle waltzed round, bobbing and spinning, and what with trying to paddle and trying to play the line, it was lob's chance whether the youth would catch the salmon or the salmon would catch him.

Anyway; at the finish, he got it over the side and into the coracle. It was a big salmon; it was that. It lay there, flapping its tail, and gasping; and he picked up the knocker to hit it on the head with. But all of a sudden it twisted and reared up against his leg, and it said, "Be my cariad."

Well, you can imagine. There he was, in the middle

63

of the river, with the knocker lifted in his hand, and the salmon said, "Be my cariad." Cariad is what you call a body in Wales when you're sweet on them; and there was the fish, talking to him, and giving him cariad!

But, "No," says the youth. "I'm going to knock you on the head." (You see he kept his wits about him.)

And the salmon says back at him, "Be my cariad; and I shall be your cariad."

"No," says he. "I'm going to knock you on the head." And he pulled back his arm to biff the salmon a good un – when that salmon gave another twist of its tail and bumped against him and fetched him down, and he landed in a heap on top of the salmon and skrawked his face on its scales. But it wasn't rightly scales any more. No. It was skin. Cold wet skin. And he found himself held tight; and he looked; and he saw there was no salmon, but a woman, with her arms fast around him and her face close against his.

"Be my cariad," she says.

"No, I will not!" says the youth. "I'll knock you on the head!"

"Then I'll drown you," she says. And she held on to him, and she hutched and thrutched, and tipped the both of them in the water.

The Salmon Cariad

She took him deep under, what's more, and then she brought him up for air.

"Be my cariad," she says.

"No, I'll not!" he says.

"Down you go," she says. And down he went!

Up again she fetched him, and he was in a poor way by now.

"Be my cariad," she says.

"No," he says.

Down they went again, into the weeds and such. Up they come.

"Be my cariad," she says, and this time he thinks he might as good wed a fish as be going up and down in the river all night; so he says, "All right," he says. "I'll be your cariad."

"Good lad," she says; and she held him up out of the water and swum him to the bank.

He grabbed and pulled himself up on the grass; but the coracle and all his gear, they were taken by the water and washed away. And he was left with this woman; well, a girl, more like, nearer his age, white as a salmon, and not a stitch on her.

She wasn't feeling too good herself, now, for she'd been hooked as a fish, and that hook was still in her, through her lip; and the rod was in the coracle yonder and being carried off by the river; so she wasn't very comfortable. She was trying to get the hook out, but

not having much success.

"Here," says the youth, for he couldn't help but pity her, "give over wriggling. I'll get the hook out."

So he did his best; but the hook was fast in.

"It's no use," he says. "It'll have to be my little knife. I must cut you."

"Ay," she says. "Cut me."

So he took his knife, and he cut the hook out; and she never budged. But as soon as that hook was free, she lifted her face to his, and she kissed him hard, right on the mouth, so that he couldn't help getting her blood on him, and tasting it, too.

"And now you've taken my blood on you," she says, "you must love me for ever."

And would you credit it, but he did love her! From that moment, he was full of love; and she loved him; and he took her home and lived with her a long and lucky life, and they had a heap of children.

Now there's not a great lot more to tell. There was one thing about them, though, that was a bit queer. Every single child that they had was born with a little white scar, or what seemed like one, on the top lip, a bit to the left. I knew one of their lads. He used to come out of Wales driving cattle to market, and it was him who told me the tale; and I've seen his scar.

Wicked Sparrow

There was a wicked sparrow and he went for a walk. After he'd hiked up and down the hills a bit, he trod on a thorn, and it stuck in his foot and made him shout.

"What's to do with you?" said a baker who heard him yelling.

"I've got a thorn in my foot," said the wicked sparrow, "and it's giving me gyp!"

"Hold still," said the baker, "and I'll take it out."

The baker took the thorn out of the wicked sparrow's foot and threw the thorn into his oven. And the wicked sparrow went on with his walk.

After a while, he came back to the baker, and he said, "Have you finished with my thorn yet?"

"I've not got your thorn," said the baker. "I burnt it in the oven."

"Who said you could burn my thorn?" said the wicked sparrow. "Give me back my thorn! I want

my thorn!" And he played heck with the baker. It was language children should not hear and grown men never use. The baker didn't know where to put himself. In the end, "Here," he said, "you take this fresh loaf, and hush up."

So the wicked sparrow took the loaf, and he went on with his walk.

He came to a flock of sheep, and the shepherds were just going to have their breakfast. They were throwing sand and soil and all sorts into their milk.

"What are you doing that for," said the wicked sparrow, "chucking muck in the milk?"

"Because we've no bread to make pobs," said the shepherds.

"I've got some bread," said the wicked sparrow.

"You can have this loaf, if you want."

"Thank you very much," said the shepherds; and they broke the loaf into the milk and had their pobs. And the wicked sparrow, he went on with his walk.

After a bit, he came that way again, and he said to the shepherds, "Have you done with my bread yet?"

"Done?" said the shepherds. "We've done, right enough! We've supped it!"

"What?" said the wicked sparrow. "Who said you could? Give me my bread! I want my bread!" And he played heck with those shepherds. It was language children should not hear and grown men never use. The shepherds didn't know what to do. "Here," said one, "you take this lamb, and let's have less of your racket."

So the wicked sparrow took the lamb, and he went on with his walk.

What should he come upon next but a wedding; and the cook was trying to catch hold of a big dog he'd got in the yard.

"What's up with you?" said the wicked sparrow. "Why are you after the big dog?"

"The butcher's out of meat," said the cook, "and we're desperate for the wedding."

"I've got a lamb," said the wicked sparrow. "You can have this lamb, if you want it."

"Thank you very much," said the cook; and he set

about roasting the lamb. And the wicked sparrow, he went on with his walk.

But he was soon back. And the wedding breakfast was still going strong.

"Have you finished with my lamb yet?" said the wicked sparrow.

"It's them who've finished with it," said the cook. "They've eaten it!"

"Eaten my lamb?" said the wicked sparrow. "Who said they could? Give me my lamb! I want my lamb!" And he played heck with the cook and the wedding guests. It was language children should not hear and grown men never use. It made the air blue and the women's faces red.

"It's no use you carrying on like that," said the bride's father. "It was a good bit of meat. Here," he said, "you take the bride, and get off with your bother. You're spoiling our fun."

So the wicked sparrow took the bride, and he went on with his walk.

But he'd not gone far when he met a man riding a donkey, and playing on a tambourine.

"Give me that tambourine," said the wicked sparrow. "I like that tambourine."

"No," said the man. "It's too dear to give away."

"You give me that tambourine," said the wicked sparrow, "and I'll give you this bride."

"Fair enough," said the man. "Swoppery's no robbery." And he gave his tambourine to the wicked sparrow and took the bride up behind him on the donkey.

The wicked sparrow went on with his walk; and he came to a tree by a river. He capered up to the top of the tree, banging the tambourine, pleased as Punch, and giving out how clever he was to have got from thorn to tambourine by way of bread, lamb and bride. He sang:

> "Oh, I am a clever lad, I am and all!
> And I am a clever lad, I am and all!
> I gave the thorn, I took the bread,
> I gave the bread, I took the lamb,

Wicked Sparrow

I gave the lamb, I took the bride,
I gave the bride, I took the
   Beautiful tambourine!
And I am a clever lad, I am and all!"

But just then he thumped that tambourine a bit too hard, and he missed his footing, and he fell in the river.

And the funny thing is, no one's seen him since.

Billy Bowker's Mowing Match

I'm going to tell you about Billy Bowker. He was a hobthrust who went boggart.

Now your hobthrust, he's the one as does the chores at night, in the house and around the farm; and all he wants for it is a saucer of milk left for him by the hearth. But your boggart, he's a great nowt. Let one of them catch hold on you, and you'll not rest in your bed; and getting rid of him's a lot easier said than done. But I'll tell you how one chap managed it.

Well, there was this hobthrust they called Billy Bowker, and he'd been on the same farm for I don't know how many years: hundreds, I shouldn't wonder; and they'd never had any trouble with him, till this summer I'm telling you about, when he starts to get above himself, cracking on that because he's fetched the hay in, mucked out the pigs and swept the kitchen, the whole blessed farm should belong to him.

The farmer couldn't have that; and he tells him; but Billy Bowker turns round and begins scolding like a cut purse! And the farmer tells him what he can do about that, too!

That puts the cat among the pigeons! Billy Bowker sets to, and he gives the farmer no peace, day and night, with rattling and banging about and smashing pots and things, same as any common or garden boggart might do: it's a morning's work, regular, to clean up after him. Then the farmer, he leaves off putting milk out for Billy, to spite him; and so it goes from bad to worse, till Billy Bowker declares that he's to be master now, and the farmer must go work for him, for a change.

The farmer and Billy, they chunner and they chunner, calling each other all the names under the sun. At last, Billy says the farmer must do the work himself, but they'll go shares, half and half, on all they get. By this time, there's not hardly a cup nor a plate left in one piece, nor a stick of furniture that's fit to be used; so the farmer gives over arguing and ploughs his field, as he's been told, and the winter passes quiet as a tater.

When spring comes, Billy Bowker says, "Time to be doing;" and the farmer goes to his shed, and says, "What shall you have, Billy? Tops or bottoms?"

"Bottoms," says Billy.

So the farmer carries out wheat seed, and plants it. And that summer, at harvest, he keeps the grain for himself, and he gives Billy Bowker the roots and stubble. "There you are, Billy," he says. "That's yours."

Next year, the farmer says to him, "What shall you have, Billy? Tops or bottoms?"

"Tops," says Billy, thinking: I'm not going to be bitten twice by the same dog, me!

But now the farmer plants turnips; and in the winter he makes a big clamp of them for himself, and Billy Bowker is left to make what he can of the leaves.

The next year, Billy Bowker says he'll have none of it: not tops or bottoms; he will not. "Corn," he says.

"You'll plant corn. And when it's ripe, we'll put a line down the middle of the field, and we'll have us a mowing match, me and you; no more of your tops or bottoms; this time, it's winner keeps all, land and crop."

So the farmer plants corn. But July next, he goes and has a word with the blacksmith; and the blacksmith, he makes the farmer ever so many thin iron rods; and the farmer plants them one night all over Billy Bowker's half of the field.

Anyway; the corn's ripe, and Billy Bowker says they must mow. So, in the morning, as soon as it's coming light, they take their scythes, and they both go to the same end of the field, and they start mowing.

The farmer marches along his patch, up and down, up and down, as clean as nip. But Billy Bowker's scythe keeps getting snagged like I don't know what, and he's blunging back and to, and doesn't hardly know which way to turn for the best.

"Mortal hard docks, these," says Billy. "Mortal hard docks."

But it's the blacksmith's iron rods as are doing it, of course. They take the edge off his scythe in no time; and Billy Bowker's flummoxed.

Now in a mowing match, the mowers must stop for sharpening up at certain times only, and they must do it both together; that's the rule. So Billy

Bowker, wanting to put the edge back on his scythe quick, he calls to the farmer, "When do we wiffle-waffle, mate?"

And the farmer, he shouts back, "Oh, about noon, mebbe!"

"Noon!" says Billy Bowker. "Then I've lost me land!" And he drops his scythe, and he runs; and he's not been seen on that farm again.

And no wonder.

Hom Bridson

There was one time a woman called Colloo, and she
had a brat of a boy that had fallen sick strangely.
Nothing seemed to be wrong with him, yet he grew
crosser and crosser, nying-nyanging night and day,
till his mother didn't know rightly where to put
herself with him.

It seems that, about a three-week after he was born,
the child – and he was a fine child; as fine as you
would see in a day's walk – he was left sleeping
while his mother went to the well for water. Now
one thing she had not done: she had not put the fire
tongs on the cradle while she was away, to keep the
child from harm; for there's all manner of things that
can hurt a new baby, if it's not made safe with a bit
of iron near it. Anyway, when she came back with
the water, the child was crying, and there was no
quietening him.

And from that instant minute the flesh seemed to

melt off his bones, till he grew as ugly and as shrivelled as a nut; and he was that way, his whining howl filling the house, lying in the cradle without a motion on him to put his feet under him. Not a day's rest nor a night's sleep was there on the woman these four years with him. She was scourged with him, until there came a fine day in the spring that Hom Bridson, the tailor, was in the house sewing. Hom was wise tremendous, for he was always from house to house with his sewing, and gathering wisdom as he went.

Well, before that day, Hom had seen lots of wickedness in the child. When his mother would be out feeding the pigs and seeing to the creatures, he would be hoisting his head up out of the cradle and making faces at Hom, winking, and slicking, and shaking his head, as if saying, "What a lad! What a lad I am!"

That day the woman wanted to go to the shop to sell some eggs that she had, and she says to Hom, "Hom, man, keep your eye on the child and see he won't fall out of the cradle, while I slip down to the shop." And when she was gone, Hom began to whistle to himself as he stitched; it was a tune he'd heard the parson singing.

"Drop that, Hom," says a voice, little and hard.

Hom was amazed. He looked to see was it the child that had spoken; and it was!

"Whush, whush, now; lie quiet," says Hom; and

he rocked the cradle with his foot and went on whistling the tune.

"Drop that, Hom, I tell you," says the brat back at him sharp, "and give us something light and handy."

"Anything at all to please you," says Hom; and he began at whistling a jig.

"Hom," says me laddo, "can you dance anything to that?"

"I can," says Hom. "Can you?"

"I can that," says me laddo. "Would you like to see?"

"I would," says Hom.

"Take that fiddle down from the wall," says me laddo, "and put the Tune of the Big Wheel on it."

"I'll do that for you, and welcome," says Hom.

So the fiddle quits its hook, and the tailor tunes up.

"Hom," says the brat, "before you begin, just you clear the kitchen for me – chairs and stools and all away. I want room to step out, man."

"I'll do that for you," says Hom.

He cleared the kitchen floor, and then he struck up the Tune of the Big Wheel.

In a crack the brat bounced from his cradle to the floor with a "Chu!" and then he was flying round the kitchen. "Go it, Hom! Face your partner! Heel and toe does it! Well done, Hom! Jog your elbow, man!" and I don't know what. Hom plays faster and faster,

82

till me laddo was jumping as high as the table.

With a "Chu!" up goes his foot on top of the dresser, and "Chu!" then on top of the chimney piece, and "Chu!" bang against the door; then he was half flying and half footing it round the kitchen, turning and going that quick that it put a reel in Hom's head to be looking at him. And Hom himself by degrees gets up on the table in the corner and plays wilder and wilder, and the whirling jig grew madder and madder.

"That's it!" shouts Hom. "I must run!" And he throws down his fiddle. "You're not the child that was in the cradle! Are you?"

"You're right enough," says me laddo. "Strike up, Hom! Make haste! Make haste, man!"

"Whush!" says Hom. "Your ma's coming!"

The dancing stopped. The brat gave a hop, skip, and a jump into the cradle.

"Get on with your sewing, Hom," he says, "and don't you say a word." And he covered himself up in the clothes till there was only his eyes to be seen, and they keeked out like a ferret's.

When the mother came in the house, Hom was sitting cross-legged on the table and his specs on his nose, letting on that he was busy sewing; and the child in the cradle was shouting and sweeling as usual.

"But it's queer stitching altogether there's been

going on here, and me out," says the woman. "And how you can see your needle in that dark corner, Hom Bridson, it beats me," she says, siding the place as she speaks. "Well, well, well, then, well, well! What is it that's doing on me darling? Did he think Mammy had gone and left him, then? Mammy is going to feed him, though."

"Look here, woman," says Hom. "Give him nothing at all, but go out and get a creelful of good turf for the fire."

She brought in the turf, and a big bart of fern on it. Hom gave a leap off the table to the floor, and it wasn't long till he had a fine glow going.

"You'll have the house put on fire for me, Hom Bridson!" she says.

"No fear, but I'll fire some of them," says Hom, and he stepped towards the cradle.

The brat, with his two eyes going out of his head watching, he was turning his whining howl into a sort of call – to his own sort to come and fetch him, like as not.

"I'll send you home," says Hom. And he stretches out his two hands to take the brat and put him on the big red turf fire. But before he's able to lay hold on him, me laddo jumps out of the cradle and takes for the door.

"The back of me hand and the side of me foot to you!" says he. "If I should only have had only another night, I could have shown you a trick or two more than that yet, Hom Bridson!"

The door flew open with a bang, as if some had thrown it open, and he took off with himself like a shot.

A great hullaballoo of laughing and making fun went up outside; shrieking, too, and running feet that were bare, by the sound of them.

Out of the door of the house goes the mother. She saw no one; but she caught sight of a flock of clouds, the shape of gulls, and low-lying, chasing each other; then she heard, as if from far off with the clouds,

sharp whistles and wicked little laughs, making mock.

And there, on the stone bench right before her, she sees her own sweet smiling boy. And she took all the joy in the world of the child that he was home again safe and sound. And she gave Hom Bridson a good tea that night.

Cocky-keeko

At some time or other, but not long since, there was an old man who kept a cat and a cock; and, one day, he set off to go working in the fields. The cat went with him to carry his bottle of tea, but he left Cocky-keeko behind to watch the house.

Just then who should come along but a fox; and he sat himself under the window and he sang a little song:

> "Cocky-keeko, Cocky-keeko?
> Gold-nob!
> Look out of the window,
> And I'll give you a bean!"

Cocky-keeko opened the window, and he stuck his head out to see who it was singing. The fox grabbed hold of him, and he carried him off.

"Oh!" shouts Cocky-keeko:

> "Cocky-keeko! Cocky-keeko!
> The fox has got Cocky-keeko!
> He'll take him through dark woods
> And into foreign parts!
> Cocky-keeko!"

The cat heard the racket, and she came rushing back and gave the fox such a clout that he dropped Cocky-keeko and ran away.

"My word, Cocky-keeko!" said the cat. "Don't you look out of the window again, do you hear? All that fox wants is to granch you up, bones and all."

Next day, the old man set off for work, and the cat went with him to carry his bottle of tea.

"Now be told," said the cat to Cocky-keeko. "And no looking out of windows."

"I shan't," said Cocky-keeko.

But no sooner had they gone than the fox came and sat himself under the window, and he sang his little song:

> "Cocky-keeko, Cocky-keeko?
> Gold-nob!
> Look out of the window,
> And I'll give you a bean;
> And I'll give you some corn!"

But Cocky-keeko didn't answer. He walked up and down. So the fox sang his little song again, and he flirted a bean in through the window. Cocky-keeko ate the bean, and he said, "You don't fool me! All you want is to granch me up, bones and all!"

"How can you say such a thing?" said the fox. "I wouldn't dream of eating you, Cocky-keeko! I've given you the bean; do you not want any corn?"

"Oh, I do!" said Cocky-keeko; and he stuck his head out of the window. The fox grabbed hold of him, and he carried him off.

"Oh!" shouts Cocky-keeko:

> "Cocky-keeko! Cocky-keeko!
> The fox has got Cocky-keeko!
> He'll take him through dark woods,
> And over rocky hills,
> And into foreign parts!
> Cocky-keeko!"

The cat heard the racket, and she came rushing back and gave the fox such a clout that he dropped Cocky-keeko and ran away.

"My word, Cocky-keeko!" said the cat. "What are we to do with you? Don't you look out of the window again, do you hear? All that fox wants is to granch you up, bones and all."

Next day, the old man set off for work, and the cat went with him to carry his bottle of tea.

"Now be told," said the cat to Cocky-keeko. "And no looking out of windows."

"I shan't," said Cocky-keeko.

But no sooner had they gone than the fox came and sat himself under the window, and he sang his little song:

91

"Cocky-keeko, Cocky-keeko?
Gold-nob!
Butter-head!
Look out of the window!
I'll give you a sack of beans!
I'll give you a sack of corn!"

But Cocky-keeko didn't answer. He walked up and down. The fox sang his little song three times; but still Cocky-keeko didn't answer; and he didn't look out of the window, neither.

"I've fetched something to show you, Cocky-keeko," said the fox.

"Oh no you haven't," said Cocky-keeko. "You'll not fool me! All you want to do is granch me up, bones and all!"

"How can you say such a thing?" said the fox. "I wouldn't dream of eating you, Cocky-keeko! I just want to show you this whim-wham from Yocketon."

"And what's that?" said Cocky-keeko.

"Do you not know?" said the fox. "I thought everybody knew! Do you really not want to see my whim-wham from Yocketon?"

"I might," said Cocky-keeko.

"Here it is, then," said the fox. "Mind you don't hurt the thrutching-piece."

"Where's that?" said Cocky-keeko; and he stuck

his head out of the window to see. The fox grabbed hold of him, and he carried him off.

"Oh!" shouts Cocky-keeko:

> "Cocky-keeko! Cocky-keeko!
> The fox has got Cocky-keeko!
> He'll take him through dark woods,
> And over rocky hills,
> And salty water,
> And into foreign parts!
> Cocky-keeko!"

But the old man was working too far distant for the cat to hear.

So the fox stopped behind the woodshed. "Quietness is best," he said, as he bit the head off Cocky-keeko; and he granched him up, bones and all, leaving the tail feathers for the wind to blow.

"Eh dear," said the old man. "There's some just won't be told."

Jack Hannaford
and the Gold to Paradise

There was an old soldier who'd been to the wars; and when he came back he hadn't a penny to his name. He set off on the tramp, and he went begging up and down, till he came to a farm one day.

Now at this farm there was living a farmer and his wife; and she'd been a widow before that. This woman, she was a born fool, and she was wearing out her second husband as fast as she'd worn the first with her stupid ways.

The day we're talking of, the farmer had gone off to market early, and before he went, he'd said to his wife, "Here's ten pound in gold. You see as you take good care of it while I get back from market." Then off he'd gone.

The wife said to herself, "I know a place for ten pound." And she wrapped the gold in a piece of rag and shoved it up the chimney. "It'll be safe there," she said.

That was when Jack Hannaford, the old soldier, came knocking at the door.

"Who is it?"

"Jack Hannaford."

"Where are you from?"

"Paradise."

"From Paradise? Then maybe you've seen my other husband!"

"Oh, I have."

"How's he doing?"

"Pretty fair: not too bad. He's a cobbler now, you know, and all he's getting to eat is cabbage."

"How's that?"

"It's what he can afford."

"Did he not give you a message?"

"He did, missis. He says can you let him have a few shillings to buy leather with? Leather's scarce there, you see, and without the leather he's got no work; and that's why he's eating so poorly."

"Bless his soul! Of course I can!" And she reached up into the chimney and pulled out the ten pounds. "You give him this," she said. "And he's to buy all the leather he needs, tell him, and he can send me back what's left."

"I must love you and leave you, missis," said Jack Hannaford. "I'm a long way from Paradise, and it gets dark early round here. I'd best be doing." And off Jack Hannaford went with the money.

Sooner or later, the farmer came back from market.

"Have you got that ten pound safe?" he said.

"It's safe enough," said the woman. "I've lent it to my other husband to buy leather with for cobbling shoes in Paradise," she said. "There was ever such a nice man here just now, and he said he'd take the ten pound to Paradise and give it him."

"Give it him? I'll give it you!" said the farmer. "You blob-tongue! You've as much wit as three folk, you have: two fools and a madman!"

"And if I have," she said, "more fool you for

96

leaving the money with me, you nazzy crow!"

The farmer got back on his horse and rode after Jack Hannaford.

But Jack Hannaford heard the horse coming, and he lay down quick by the hedgeside, on his back, one hand shading his eyes, and pointing at the sky with the other.

Up galloped the farmer, all of a dither-a-wack, like a new-baked custard; but he was forced to stop when he saw the picture Jack Hannaford was making.

"What are you playing at down there?"

"By the cringe, master! But I've seen a rare sight!"

"What have you seen?"

"A man going straight up into the sky, same as if he was on a road; and he's carrying something in a bit of rag!"

"Can you still see him?"

"I should say so!"

"Where is he?"

"You get down here, master, and you'll see for yourself!"

The farmer got down from his horse, and he lay on his back in the road, skenning up at the sky.

"I can't see him," he said.

"Just you keep looking," said Jack Hannaford, "and before very long you'll see a man moving away from you as fast as he can go."

And he did, too! He saw Jack Hannaford jumping up on the horse's back and riding off with both horse and gold!

The farmer, he had to walk home.

"You great gawpsheet!" said his wife. "What did I tell you? You're the big fool, not me! I've done only one daft thing; and now you've gone and done two!"

And there wasn't a lot he could say at her, after that.

Todlowery

An old man and an old woman lived in an old house. One day, as he was eating his beans, a bean dropped out of the old man's spoon and rolled into a crack in the floor; and it began to grow. It grew and it grew. It grew till it reached the sky.

The old man said, "Whatever next?" And he started off up the beanstalk to the sky. When he got to the top, he looked all around him, and he said, "I'll fetch the old woman up to see this lot. It will suit her a treat."

He climbed back down to the ground, and he put the old woman in a bag, and the bag between his teeth, and he climbed up again.

As he climbed, the old woman said, "Are we there, yet?" But the old man said nothing, and went on climbing. "Are we there, yet?" said the old woman a while later. The old man said nothing, and went on climbing. The old woman waited; and then she said,

"Man, are we there, yet?" "Hush," he said. "You're an unpatient woman." But at that the bag slipped from between the old man's teeth and fell all the way down to the ground, and the old woman was killed dead.

Well, the old man had to set about burying the old woman then; and the first thing he had to do was to find a mourner for the funeral. So he put three pair of white chickens in the bag the old woman had been in, and he went out to look for a mourner.

He met a bear. "Bear," he said, "can you be a mourner for the old woman? I'll give two white chickens, if you can."

"Oh, I can," said the bear.

"Let's hear you."

"Oh, granny!" said the bear. "How I mourn for you!"

"That won't do," said the old man; and he went on his way till he met a wolf. "Wolf," said the old man, "can you be a mourner for the old woman? I'll give two white chickens, if you can."

"Oh, I can," said the wolf.

"Let's hear you."

"Oh, granny!" said the wolf. "How I mourn for you!"

"That won't do," said the old man; and he went on his way till he met Todlowery the fox. "Todlowery," said the old man, "can you be a mourner for the old woman? I'll give two white chickens, if you can."

"Oh, I can," said Todlowery.

"Let's hear you."

So Todlowery started to cry, and he rubbed his eyes with his paws, and he sang:

> "Turu! Turu, ma! Turu!
> The old man's done for you!
> Turu! Turu, ma! Turu!"

"That's grand," said the old man. "Here's two chickens. Now, for another two, just let me hear the fine words again."

So Todlowery wept, and sang again:

> "Turu! Turu, ma! Turu!
> The old man's done for you!
> Turu! Turu, ma! Turu!"

"Here's two chickens," said the old man. "Now let's hear it again."

So Todlowery wept, and sang again, and the old man gave him two chickens, and he asked Todlowery to sing yet again; and Todlowery wept and sang a fourth time. But then the old man saw that he had no more chickens in his bag.

"I've left the pair at home," he said. "Will you come with me?"

Todlowery

"I'll come with you," said Todlowery. So they went together to the old man's house, and the old man took the bag, and put in a pair of dogs, and covered them with the six white chickens, and gave the bag to Todlowery.

Todlowery took the bag and ran off with it. He came to a tree stump, and he sat down. "I could just eat two white chickens," he said. So he did. He went on, and he came to another stump, and he sat down and ate two more white chickens. At a third stump, he ate a third pair. And at a fourth stump, he sat down and said, "One more pair will do me fine." He opened the bag; and out jumped the old man's dogs, barking.

Todlowery ran. And he ran. He ran and he ran. He ran till he could run no more. Then he hid under a log; and Todlowery said:

"Little ears, little ears, what do you do?"
"We listen, we listen, lest the dogs eat the fox."
"Little eyes, little eyes, what do you do?"
"We watch, we watch, lest the dogs eat the fox."
"Little legs, little legs, what do you do?"
"We run, we run, lest the dogs eat the fox."
"Little tail, little tail, what do you do?"
"I tangle bush, briar and wood,
    so the dogs catch the fox."

"Oh, wicked tail!" said Todlowery. "If that be so, here, dogs! Eat it!"

And Todlowery stuck out his tail from under the log; and the dogs grabbed it, and pulled out the fox, and ate him. And that was the end of Todlowery.

Johnny Whopstraw and the Hare

Johnny Whopstraw was out walking one fine day when he spied a hare sitting under a bush on a common. He thought: What luck! Here's me; and I'll catch this hare, and I'll kill him with a whip, and then I'll sell him for half-a-crown. With that money, I can get a young sow, I reckon; and I'll feed her up on scraps, and she'll bring me twelve piglets.

The piglets, when they're grown, they'll have twelve piglets each. And when they're grown, I'll slaughter the lot of them; and that'll bring me a barn-load of pork.

I'll sell the pork, and I'll buy a little house for my mother to live in; and then I can get married myself.

I'll marry a farmer's daughter; and she'll fetch the farm with her. We'll have two sons; and I'll work

them hard and pay them little. They'll be that whacked, they'll oversleep in the morning, and I'll have to give them a shout to rouse them. "Get up, you lazy beggars!" I'll say. "The cows want milking!"

But Johnny Whopstraw had fallen so in love with his big ideas that he really did shout, "Get up, you lazy beggars! The cows want milking!"

And that hare, it took fright at the row he was making, and it ran off across the common; and he never did catch it; and his money, pigs, house, wife, farm and children were lost, all because of that.

Belenay of the Lake

Let's see if I can remember it all as it was told to me.

Once long ago, in the golden holiness of a night, that will never be again and never will come back, there was, old time, a young man called Hewin, and he lived with his mother on a farm by the side of a lake.

Young Hewin looked out, this night that I'm telling you, and he saw a woman; she was on the water, sitting, she was, and combing her long yellow hair in the moonlight.

He went to the shore of the lake, Hewin, and he said to her, "Beautiful girl, come here! Oh, you beauty!" He felt in his pocket for something to give her, but all he'd got was an old crust of bread. That will have to do, he thought; so he held it out to her.

But she went on combing her yellow hair, and she said to him:

"Hard is your bread,
And not easy to win me."

Then she went; she vanished; she was gone.

Well, Hewin went back to the house and told his mother. "Mam," he says, "the crust was too hard. If I don't get her, I don't know what I'll do."

"You take her a batch of dough tomorrow," says his mother; "and then we'll see about too hard."

110

Next night, the woman was sitting on the water, combing her hair, and Hewin went down with his batch of dough. He held it out to her, and he said, "Beauty girl, come here, do!"

But she went on combing her hair, and she said:

> "Unbaked is your bread,
> And won't win me."

And again she was gone; just like that.

Hewin told his mother. "I don't know what to do, Mam," he says.

"Never you mind," she says. "Third time pays for all."

That same night, his mother baked him a loaf; and in the morning, at sunrise, Hewin went down and held out the new loaf of bread. "Beauty girl," he says, "come here! Come here, do!"

Then she rose up in the water, the young woman, and came towards him; and she said:

> "Well is your bread,
> And you shall win me."

Hewin was glad, I can tell you!

She came out of the water. "Belenay shall be a wife to you," she says, "until the day you hit her with a piece of iron; and on that day she shall leave you."

"I'll not hit you at all," says Hewin; "with iron, or

without. I shall never!"

She said nothing to that, and they went up to the house to see his mother. And behind them, out from the lake, ten cows followed; and four oxen; and a white bull! They came from under the water, for a dowry, like, for Belenay; Hewin's mother said it was quite the thing!

So Hewin and Belenay were married that night, and were very happy.

By and by, they had three sons, one after the other. The farm was going well, too, with the cows keeping their promise with the milk and the butter, and the oxen ploughing the fields so that the land did seven times better than it had ever done before. It was a good time.

Well, the years passed. The children were growing. Then one morning in spring, Hewin saw a wild horse beside the lake. Well! He wasn't the man to let the chance go!

"Here, quick!" he says to Belenay. "You catch him, while I get the bridle!"

So he dashed into the house, for the bridle, and she ran along the shore after the horse; the horse galloped off, but she caught him and she twisted her fingers into his mane.

Hewin came out with the bridle, and, "Here you are!" he says; and he threw the bridle, meaning to

land it over the horse's head. But he missed, and the iron of the bridle hit Belenay on her hand.

She gave a queer bit of a cry, and let go of the mane. "Hewin, love!" she says. "That was the blow! That was the blow of iron!"

"No!" says Hewin. "Don't leave me!"

"I can't stay!" she says.

"What about the children?" he says.

"I must go!" she says. "I must!"

She was walking down to the lake, looking back over her shoulder, and into the water; and then she started to sing, in her high, clear voice that she used to call the cattle in, and oh, it was a strange song!

> "Mulican, Molican, Malen, Mair,
> Come you home to my word!
> Brindled cow, white speckled,
> Spotted cow, broad freckled,
> Hornless Dodin, Yellow Anvil,
> Stray Horns, and the Grey Geingen,
> With the white bull
> From the court of the king,
> And the oxen on the field,
> And the black calf on the hook,
> All come home to my word!"

And the cattle answered her, lowing and bellowing, and they did come to her; even the freshly killed calf from the hook, he came; and the bull that was tethered by the nose, he pulled out the ring stake and followed; and the oxen that were ploughing, they came, dragging the plough after them – and there's still the mark of the furrow to be seen, from the field to the water, if you'll look. All in one line they followed her.

That's how it was. Belenay took back with her under the water all that she'd brought from it. And at the spot where she went into the water, where the lake had filled her very last footprint, a single white lily grew.

Hewin never saw Belenay again. He called, and he called, and he walked by the lakeside day and night, till he grew old and he died; but he never saw her. The blow of iron had parted them.

But the boys, that was different. The three of them, they would often go down on the bright nights of the moon and stand at the white lily and call to their mother. And she would answer them from the water. They used to talk together, all four, and Belenay would teach them what there was to be known of healing and of herbs, so that they grew to be wise men and doctors.

It was hard for Hewin. But that's how it was, old time.

Alice of the Lea

Now this is an old tale the Cornishmen brought out of Cornwall with them, when they came getting copper in the mine holes hereabouts. I recollect old Perrin used to tell it.

Anyway, it seems there was this girl: Alice of the Lea, she was called. Her father was dead, and her mother had only her; there were no brothers or sisters; just Alice. Oh, but she was bonny! She was tall and fair skinned, yet with black, raven hair; a perfect picture; but it was her eyes that struck you, so that, once you'd seen them, you'd never forget them: big, and blue, they were, like the sea. And she lived in a big castle; just her and her mother, and the servants to look after them both.

Of course, lots of young men came courting, but Alice would have none of them. No; her heart was set on one man: Bevil of Stowe; that was his name; and he was a grand figure of a knight, too. But, as

116

often happens, he was the one chap who never came courting young Alice, and she was very put out by this; and so was her mother.

Well, it got to the time of year when banquets and balls and such were the thing; and Alice's mother, she thought it would be a good idea to have a ball for Alice and to invite the gentry from all around, and for the top man to be Bevil of Stowe. Alice was delighted. "If he comes," she said, "I promise you he'll have eyes only for me."

So it was given out that there was to be a ball for Alice, and the gentry said they'd come, and Bevil of Stowe said he'd be there, too; which was all that Alice and her mother were after.

The castle was got ready. Floors were scrubbed; walls were whitewashed; windows were cleaned; chimneys were swept; decorations were put up; every sort of food and drink was fetched in; while Alice and her mother were here, there and everywhere, ordering this, and ordering that, till the servants didn't know whether they were coming or going. Then, when all was natty, Alice went up to her room, shut herself in, and wouldn't let anybody near her for two days, not even her mother; not even on the night of the ball itself, she wouldn't.

The guests were arriving, and still Alice kept herself in her room. Her mother went and knocked on the

door and asked: "Are you ready, Alice?" she said.

"No, I'm not," said Alice.

"The gentry's come," said her mother.

"Is Bevil of Stowe here yet?" said Alice.

"No, not yet," said her mother.

"Tell me when he is," said Alice.

So her mother had to go down and look after the guests, while Alice stayed in her room. They must have wondered what was up.

Anyway, it wasn't long before Bevil of Stowe put in his appearance; and he was looking well. Alice's mother ran upstairs and knocked on her door.

"He's here, Alice!" she said. "He's come!"

"Then I'm ready," said Alice; and she opened the door.

Well, you never saw such a gorgeous sight as Alice when she opened that door. Her mother was thunderstruck; flabbergasted, she was.

Alice stood there; an amethyst ring on her finger, amethysts in her hair; a brooch of one great amethyst on her breast; and she was in a dress all of black velvet. And ring, amethysts, brooch, black velvet and all, were there to set off the marvel of her blazing blue eyes.

"Oh, Alice!" said her mother. "I pray that Bevil of Stowe shall bend his soul when he sees you now. I

119

pray that you shall get his love tonight; and the wedding to follow fast; that's what I'll pray."

"Pray?" says Alice. "What good's praying? With these eyes, and this dress, what chance has Bevil of Stowe? No, mother. Blue eyes and black velvet: they're more than any prayer!"

And as she stood in her highness and spoke those words, there came a sound like a rushing wind, and a flash of fire, a sweet smell, and a wild music. Then nothing. And where was Alice of the Lea? Vanished. Gone. And that for ever.

Oh, they sought her up and down; north, south, east and west; day and night they sought her. But she wasn't found. And at last they gave up looking.

Years passed. Alice's mother grew feeble, and died heartbroken. The castle fell. People forgot. Only a few old women remembered, and then not clearly. The castle stones were carted off for mending roads; and the land was ploughed up and turned to pasture.

Then, one day, a farmer, going milking, spotted a little hillock of fresh earth standing out against the green grass. He turned it over with his boot; and he saw something glinting in the earth. He picked it up; and it was a ring; an amethyst ring; her ring! Alice of the Lea's; the one she was wearing that night! And inside the ring were some words written in the gold; words in the old Cornish twang. They said:

"Beryan Erde,
Oyn und Perde."

That's what they said. And it was a while before any could tell what it meant, for all that had been forgotten long since. But they did find one old chap who still spoke the twang; and he read it off for them:

"Earth must hide
Both eyes and pride."

Well, what were they to make of that? The old chap read it off again:

"Earth must hide
Both eyes and pride."

And just then, they all heard the sound of sobbing, ever so soft, and tiny, under the ground, and a long way off. And they looked down; and there in the heap of soil they saw something move: a little black thing, it was, all in a velvet skin, like Alice's gown; and it seemed to have no eyes, and yet be scared of the light, for it burrowed down into the hillock, and they saw it no more.

And that, old Perrin used to say, was the first mole ever seen in Cornwall. Ay. Alice of the Lea. So remember:

"Beryan Erde,
Oyn und Perde."

And don't you forget it.

Harry-cap
and the Three Brothers

Jack and his two brothers were chopping down trees once, when the oldest brother said, "Cob this for a game!" he says. "I'm off to find better days." And he set down his axe and left the other two to fend for themselves, while he went to seek his fortune.

He walked and he walked, until he was dead beat, and he sat himself down on a hillside to rest. He was just nodding off to sleep, when a little man, as short as old sticks, came up to him and says, "Here, who are you? What are you doing? Where are you going?"

"I'm resting," he says. "And then I'm going looking for better days."

"Well," says the little man, "if you keep on, straight over these hills, you'll come to a white house. Say to them who are there that Harry-cap sent you; and you'll not be wasting your time."

"I'll do that," he says.

So on he walked, over the hills, and he came to a white house; and them who were there said to him, "What do you want? Where are you from?"

"Harry-cap told me to come," he says.

"Oh, well then; if Harry-cap has sent you, come in and make yourself at home!"

And they took him in, and gave him his supper, and a good wash, and they wouldn't hear of him going any further that night, but he must stop with them and sleep in a proper bed.

He slept well, too, and next morning, as he was for making tracks to be on his way, they gave him a leather purse. "You have this purse," they said, "and you'll find you'll never want for money."

He looked in the purse, and there was one gold sovereign lying in it; and that was all.

"Think on," they said; "there'll always be a piece of money in that purse, enough for what you need, neither more nor less."

Well, he thanked them, and went his way; but, after a bit, he thought there was not much use in going further. "For I've got my fortune here," he says. "I might as good go home."

And he turned round and set off back.

It was coming on dark long before he reached home, and he thought he'd treat himself that night; so he stopped off at an inn, and had him a good feed last thing, before he went to bed; and he paid for it out of the purse.

What he didn't know was that the landlord's daughter who served him his supper, she was by way of being something of a witch, and she knew what sort of a purse that was when she saw it. And that night, while he slept, she crept into his room, took his purse, and left another one, looking just like it, in its place; and the fause monkey even put the price of his breakfast in this other purse, so as he wouldn't think anything was wrong in the morning, and he'd be well on his road before he found different.

Next day, he paid for his breakfast, and by nightfall he was home; and his brothers were still mauling with chopping down trees.

"Come and see what I've got," he says, "and fetch the neighbours."

"Now," he says, when they were all in the house, "you tell me what it is you'd like to have, and I'll give you the money for it."

"I could do with a new hat," says Jack.

"I'd like a new pair of britches," says the other brother.

And the neighbours all said what they wanted to have.

"You shall have it," he says. "The money's in here."

But when he opened the purse it was empty. And the neighbours, they winked and blinked like ducks in thunder, and went away, laughing.

"Well," says the second brother, "I think I'll go looking for better days, too. I reckon I can't do worse than him." And next morning, he set off to seek his fortune.

It went the same for him as it had for the oldest. He was on the tramp all day, and sat down to rest on a hillside, and Harry-cap came and asked him what he was doing, and he told him, and Harry-cap sent him to find the white house.

They took him in, and gave him his tea and a bed for the night, and first thing they sat him down at a

little round table, and they said, "What will you have for your breakfast?"

"Oh," he says; "ham and eggs."

As soon as he spoke, a sizzling hot plate of ham and eggs appeared out of nowhere. It was that sort of a table. Anything he wanted to eat, he had only to say, and there it was before him.

So he had his breakfast and thanked them, tucked the table under his arm, and went on to seek his fortune.

Now the table, though it wasn't heavy, it was awkward, and he soon got tired of carrying it. "And besides," he says, "it's as good as a fortune. I'd be best at home, not traipsing round with a table."

He turned round and set off back. And with night coming on he arrived at the same inn where the first brother had stayed.

He told the innkeeper he wasn't hungry; he just wanted a bed, he said; and he carried the table upstairs to his room, locked the door, sat himself down, and says to the table, "Roast beef and potatoes and Yorkshire pudding." And there they were, piping hot, and the gravy, too.

But the innkeeper's daughter, the one who was a witch, she'd seen the table on the way in, and she knew what it was for. And she'd crept up, after, and was looking through the keyhole when he had his supper.

That night, when he was asleep, she swopped the table for another like it; it had the same looks, but none of its tricks. And in the morning, he paid his bill, and left, lummoxing the useless table up hill and down dale, and he got back home with the thing just before tea.

"Come and see what I've got," he says; "and fetch the neighbours." And he took the table into the house and set it down on the floor. Jack and the oldest

brother came in, with the neighbours following, and the second brother says, "What would you like for your teas?"

"A bacon butty," says Jack.

"A plate of black seam" says the oldest, "with plenty of pepper and vinegar."

"Then all you do is ask," says the second brother. "The table does the rest."

So they asked, Jack and the oldest did; and the neighbours put in their bids, too; but, of course, nothing happened. And the neighbours, they winked and blinked like ducks in thunder, and went away, laughing.

"Now then," says Jack; "it looks like you've flown high and let in a cow-clap at last. I must go see if I can't do as good."

And Jack set off to seek his fortune.

He sat down on the very same hillside, and along came Harry-cap and sent him to the white house, same as he'd done the others. And them that were there fed him and bedded him and sent him away next morning with a good, stout stick in his hand to help him on his road.

"And if you should meet any trouble," they said, "from vagabonds and such, what you do is to say to the stick, 'Stick! Thump 'em!' and your worries will be over."

So Jack set off; and when it was fetching night, he came to the inn where his brothers had stayed. He had his supper, and went to bed, leaving the stick where he could see it, on the windowsill.

He blew the candle out, and lay there on his bed, plundering in his mind what he should do to find himself better days, and he was just about to drop off to sleep, when he saw a hand come in at the window and take hold of the stick. It was the innkeeper's daughter, and she was keen to get that stick.

"Eh up!" says Jack. "Stick! Thump 'em!"

And the stick wriggled like a snig in a bottle and began at the innkeeper's daughter, and it thrashed her in through the window and round the room, and gave her the hiding of her life. And Jack wouldn't tell it to leave off till she said she'd fetch him a table and a purse that were magic, if only he'd stop the stick

from giving her such a hiding.

So Jack told the stick to stop, and the innkeeper's daughter went and got the table and the purse and handed them over; and Jack told her what he'd do if he ever saw her and her hanky-panky again. Then, in the morning, he set off home, stick in his hand, purse in his pocket, and table on his shoulder.

When he got home, Jack told his brothers to go and invite the neighbours round for a bite to eat. The neighbours came, and Jack sat them down at the table and fed them all big cream teas, with cakes and all the trimmings. Then he took out the purse and gave each of them a golden guinea.

"There," says Jack. "You've had a portion of what my brothers got; would you like to have some of what I found on my travels, now, for being such good neighbours and all?"

"Oh yes!" they said, winking and blinking like ducks in thunder. "Oh, we would! We'd like that very much!"

"Right you are," says Jack. "Then you shall have it. Stick! Thump 'em!"

The stick set about those neighbours and gave them what for. And then it drove them out of the house, down the road and over the bridge; that's what it did: out of the house, down the road and over the bridge; till the bridge bended, and my tale's ended.

A Bag of Moonshine

"Come here, lad, and I'll tell thee a tale:

I'll tell thee a tale
About a weasel and a snail,
A monkey and a merry abbot:
Seven good sons for winding.
They rambled and they romped,
And they come to a quickthorn hedge.
E'en the millstones we're going to jump in!
What must I do to save my shins?
O'er Rinley-Minley Common,
Up starts a red hare
With a good sort of a salmon feather in its tail.
Having a good broadsword by my side,
I shot at it.
No matter o' that, but I missed it.
Up comes Peter Pilkison
Mowing oat cakes in the field of Robert Tellison.
Hearing this news, he come;

A Bag of Moonshine

Tumbled o'er th' turfcote,
O'er th' backerlash,
O'er Winwick church steeple;
Drowned in a bag of moonshine
Behind Robert Chent's door,
Chowbent."

Loppy Lankin

They say that, once upon a time, in such and such a place, not near and not far, not high and not low, there lived an old man and an old woman by the side of a lake. And they had no children; but they did want a child; especially the old woman; she did want one. She was carrying on no end, until one day her husband lost patience with her, and he went into the wood, and he broke off a whippy green branch from an oak tree, and he took it home, and he wrapped it in a cloth, and he put it in a cradle and he said, "There," he says, "that's your baby for you. Get on with rearing that!" And off he went to work.

Well, the old woman, she sang hushieby songs to this whippy branch, and washed it, and cuddled it, and talked to it, and I don't know what. And this went on for some time, until the old man wished he'd never had anything to do with it; for his supper wasn't ready when he came in at night, and his clothes wanted mending; but all his wife would do was nurse this oak branch. She did love it so. She loved it, and she loved it – and she loved it into life, she did! It began to grow. And it grew into a young youth. He was talking at three months old, and walking at four; and they called him Loppy Lankin, for him being so long, and grown from the wood and all.

The old man made him a boat, and Loppy liked nothing so much as to go fishing every day in his boat on the lake. And his mother used to take him his milk, and call to him:

> "Loppy, Loppy, little lad!
> Come to your mammy,
> She's fetched your milk!"

And Loppy used to sail to the shore, drink his milk, and get on with his fishing.

Now there was a witch in those parts, and she saw Loppy fishing every day, and she thought she would have him for her dinner. So she went down to the lake, and she called, in her horrid voice:

> "Loppy, Loppy, little lad!
> Come to your mammy,
> She's fetched your milk!"

But Loppy said:

"Sail further, further, little boat!
That's no mammy,
But a wicked witch!"

And the boat sailed further out on the lake, and the
witch smacked her chops, and she went off to the
blacksmith, and, "Blacksmith," she says, "make me a
voice like Loppy Lankin's mother's."

"Right," says the blacksmith. "Let's be having your
neck on my anvil, and then."

So the witch put her neck on the blacksmith's
anvil, and the blacksmith hammered her a new voice,
straight off, just like Loppy Lankin's mother's. And

when he'd done that, the witch went back to the lake with her new voice, and called, this time ever so nicely:

"Loppy, Loppy, little lad!
Come to your mammy,
She's fetched your milk!"

And Loppy said:

"Sail closer, closer, little boat!
That's my mammy,
With my milk!"

And the boat sailed in to the shore; and the witch took Loppy and ran off with him to her house. When she got there, she gave Loppy to her daughter for her to roast while she went off to get more wood for the fire.

"Where shall you do for your roasting?" Loppy said to the daughter when the witch had gone.

"I'll use the oven," says the daughter.

"I'm too long to fit in the oven," says Loppy.

"No, you're not," says the daughter.

"Yes, I am," he says.

"I'll measure you," she says. And she upped and measured him, then she went to the oven to measure that.

"It's no good measuring outside," says Loppy. "Inside's where you want to measure."

"True," says the daughter, and she opened the oven door and reached inside. Up jumped Loppy, quick as a flash, and pushed her in, and shut the door on her.

Then he ran out of the house and climbed a tree, to watch; and he waited.

Back came the witch with her firewood and put it on the fire. And when the oven had roasted, she ate and she drank, and then she came out into the yard, where she rolled and wallowed, and she said:

> "I roll and I wallow,
> For gobbling Loppy Lankin!"

But Loppy said from the tree:

"Roll, witch! Wallow, witch!
For gobbling your daughter!"

The witch heard him, and she lifted up her head and looked all around, but she saw no one; so she said:

"I roll and I wallow,
For gobbling Loppy Lankin!"

And Loppy said from the tree:

"Roll, witch! Wallow, witch!
For gobbling your daughter!"

And the witch was frightened. And she looked up; and she saw Loppy in the tree.

That did it! The witch ran off to the blacksmith, and, "Blacksmith," she says, "make me an axe, quick!"

So, the blacksmith made the witch an axe on his anvil; but when he gave it to her, he said, "Now think on, missis," he says. "You're to chop with the butt; you mustn't chop with the edge: it'll blunt."

And would you credit it, but that witch did as he said! She ran to the tree, and began at hacking it with the butt; and of course that did her no good at all. So she threw away the axe, and began at gnawing the tree with her teeth. Now that was more like! She bit and she bit; and the tree cracked. Grey geese flew in the sky. Loppy saw the geese; and he saw it was time for him to be doing to shift himself out of that; so he said:

"Now then, geese, grey geese!
Let's be having wings under me!
And my father and my mother,
They'll give you food and drink!"

But the geese saw the witch, and they said, "Get another flock, hungrier than us, to take you home." And on they flew.

By this time, the witch was making splinters fly, never mind geese, with her chomping; and the tree shook, and cracked some more. And another flock of geese came by.

"Eh up!" says Loppy:

"Now then, geese, grey geese!
Let's be having wings under me!
And my father and my mother,
They'll give you food and drink!"

But the geese said, "There's a little bald goose following us. Maybe she'll take you." And on they flew. And the little bald goose didn't come. And the tree was bending and cracking, and the witch was

licking her lips between bites; and Loppy was thinking: Well, this won't do! when up comes the little
bald goose, and Loppy says:

"Now then, goose, little goose,
Bald goose, now then!
Let's be having wings under me!
And my father and my mother,
They'll give you food and drink;
And they'll wash you in clean water, too!"

And the little bald goose flew down and took
Loppy on her wings, just at the very moment that the